Praise for
DOUGLAS EVANS'S
Math Rashes and Other Classroom Tales

"Homework makes no sense to Hari. Consequently, he eagerly trades one of his five senses to a gnome for doing his lessons. That arrangement works well—until he unwittingly trades away his common sense. The jungle gym, the teeter-totter, and other equipment turn tables on the playground bully; and a mealworm named Bob helps a little girl spell accurately. These are only a few of the wacky takeoffs on third-grade experiences that will have readers laughing out loud. Cleverly disguising lessons on good school behavior in plays on words, fantasy, and humor, these imaginative stories delightfully re-create recognizable school situations and characters."

—*Booklist*

"The third graders at the W. T. Melon Elementary School inhabit a very real world, one that children will recognize, peopled with kids facing all sorts of problems in imaginative ways. This is one sweet, funny, and accessible book. Kids will laugh every time the tall teacher's ears turn red when he gets mad, and take comfort in the fact that they are not alone."

—*Children's Literature*

"In a world in which adults are identified by description (tall teacher, Playground Lady) or silly names (Mr. Principle the principal, Miss Givings the substitute, Mr. Leeks the custodian), these school stories unfold with an intriguing mix of fantasy and reality. Each well-written short selection has strong child appeal and is sprinkled with Di Fiori's appealing black-and-white illustrations. Recognizable characters and situations and zany plots will pull young readers in and convey gentle messages."

—*School Library Journal*

Other Signature Titles

Afternoon of the Elves
Janet Taylor Lisle

Bad Girls
Cynthia Voigt

The Classroom at the End of the Hall
Douglas Evans

The Music of Dolphins
Karen Hesse

Out of the Dust
Karen Hesse

P.S. Longer Letter Later
Ann M. Martin and Paula Danziger

Somewhere in the Darkness
Walter Dean Myers

MATH RASHES
and Other Classroom Tales

Douglas Evans

Pictures by
Larry Di Fiori

SCHOLASTIC
Signature

an imprint of
Scholastic Inc.

New York Toronto London Auckland Sydney
Mexico City New Delhi Hong Kong Buenos Aires

For Grant Evans

ISBN 0-439-33902-2

Text copyright © 2000 by Douglas Evans.
Illustrations copyright © 2000 by Larry Di Fiori. All rights reserved.
Published by Scholastic Inc., 555 Broadway, New York, NY 10012,
by arrangement with Front Street Books, Inc. SCHOLASTIC and associated
logos are trademarks and/or registered trademarks of Scholastic Inc.

24 23 22 21 20 19 18   7 8 9 10/0

Printed in the U.S.A.   40

First Scholastic printing, October 2001

Designed by Helen Robinson

Contents

The New-School-Year Moon

"It hung over the school last night like a big white period," said Mr. Leeks, the school janitor. He stood by the front door polishing the brass name plate: W. T. MELON ELEMENTARY SCHOOL.

Morgan clutched her new lunchbox. Danny shuffled in his new sneakers.

"What did?" asked Kate. "What hung over our school?"

Mr. Leeks pointed toward the sky. "The full moon of September," he said. "The New-School-Year Moon, it's called. The moon that shines over every school the night before it opens. And last night the New-School-Year Moon shone over this school brighter than ever."

Richard scratched his new haircut. Hari hung his thumbs on the straps of his new backpack.

"I'm telling you, youngsters, moonbeams lit up the playground," Mr. Leeks went on. "And while I was watching, one moonbeam, moving slower than glue, flowed up these steps and right through the front door of the school."

Joey stuffed his hands in the pockets of his new jeans.

The janitor rubbed his raspy chin before continuing. "And would you believe, that shaft of light oozed down the hallway, leaving a skinny white line across my clean floor. It passed the office and gym. It came out and entered the music room. Came out and slithered around the library. Then, don't you know, the silver beam slid under the door of *that* classroom, the one down there at the end of the hall."

"That's our classroom," said Mimi. "We're in third grade."

"We'll be in the classroom at the end of the hall this year," Andrew added.

The custodian looked at the third-graders hard. "Then, youngsters, there's something else I better tell you. There's something even more odd about the moon last night. You see, it changed."

"Changed?" said George.

"Like how?" asked Kate.

"I'm telling you, one moment I saw the familiar Man-in-the-Moon face. And the next, well, the next moment I saw a different face, the face of a man you've all seen many times before."

"Who?" asked Gabrielle.

8

"When? Where?"

Mr. Leeks turned and pointed into the school. In a voice so low it was almost a whisper, he said, "I saw the same face that's in the painting hanging  in the hallway." He pulled out his rag and resumed polishing the bronze sign.

"W. T. Melon?" the third-graders said in unison.

The custodian nodded slowly. "You're darn tootin'," he said. "The face on the New-School-Year Moon last night belonged to Walter Teach Melon himself. Gave me the willies, it did."

RIIIIIIIIIIIIIIIIIING!

Mr. Leeks opened the front door. "Time to go to your classroom, youngsters," he said. "Time to hit the books, study hard, get cracking on the lessons. And who knows, you might see changes too around the school real soon. It's happened before. Youngsters go through this door in September and come out *different* in June. Just like the New-School-Year Moon last night. Now get. Hope you have yourselves a fine school year."

Doodles

Andrew sat at his desk in the classroom at the end of the hall. Doodle rockets and doodle race cars filled the top margin of his math sheet. A doodle penguin and pirate's flag decorated the bottom. Down the right side ran doodle cubes, springs, and arrows. Down the left appeared doodle designs, mazes, and goofy faces. But despite all this artwork bordering Andrew's paper, only five of his multiplication problems were finished.

In the front of the room, the tall teacher looked up from his large metal desk. "Andrew, get busy," he called out. "Let's start working."

Andrew nodded. He filled in two more answers before doodling a vampire with fangs dripping blood in the upper corner.

"Stop wasting time, Andrew," called the teacher. "If that math work isn't completed by recess, you'll stay inside doing it."

Andrew counted the remaining problems. "Let's see, I have seven minutes to do twenty more problems," he told himself. "That's ... let's see, seven times sixty is four hundred and twenty seconds divided by twenty. That's only twenty-one seconds per problem. How can I ever get all this math done in that time?"

After answering three more problems, Andrew started doodling again. This time he drew his favorite doodle, one that appeared on all his papers and notebooks, a beast with five arms, three legs, and two heads.

When the recess bell rang, the tall teacher strolled back to Andrew's desk. He took one look at his math paper and scowled. "Andrew, why can't you ever get your work done on time?"

Andrew answered with a shrug.

"First you putter around at the pencil sharpener," the teacher went on. "Next you dawdle getting back to your desk. And those doodles, Andrew. What's with all those doodles?"

Andrew raised his palms for another answer.

The tall teacher's ears turned red. "Andrew, you'll remain at this desk until you've caught up on your work. Understand? First, finish that math. Then do the handwriting and adjective worksheets from this morning, and the spelling. And you still haven't turned in your story from yesterday."

With that, the teacher grabbed his coffee mug and left the room.

Andrew blew out his cheeks and lifted his desktop. He pulled out the half-finished handwriting paper, the adjective worksheet, the spelling book, and his story with only two lines written.

"How did I get so far behind?" he muttered to himself. He managed to do two more problems before doodling a Cyclops on the cover of his spelling book.

The recess minutes ticked away. Perhaps Andrew would have doodled the entire time if a loud whistle hadn't startled him. He paused to listen. Yes, someone very close was whistling "Yankee Doodle."

Andrew squinted at his math sheet. Was he seeing things? Every doodle on the paper was now moving. The pirate flag fluttered. The doodle springs coiled and uncoiled. The doodle race car's tires spun, and the doodle jets dropped doodle bombs that made doodle explosions at the bottom of the page.

Andrew fell back in his chair. "Doodle cartoons," he said under his breath. "This can't be happening." He checked the paper again. "But it is!"

At that moment, his favorite doodle, the three-legged, five-armed, two-headed beast, bent forward.  As it did so, its two heads rose right out of the paper. The five arms flapped and emerged as well. After the doodle's three legs advanced, the entire figure was standing on Andrew's desktop. Although still resembling a pencil cartoon—lead-colored with scribbly skin—the creature appeared three-dimensional and strutted about the math paper as if alive.

The beast turned, and two of its hands waved to Andrew.

"How ya doing, mate?" said the head on the right side. "Me name's Dilly."

The one on the left said, "My name's Dally. And we're ready to start doing your schoolwork."

Andrew's eyes widened. "Dilly-Dally?" he exclaimed. A grin spread across his face. "You mean you'll do my work for me?"

The doodle creature paced across the math paper with all five hands behind its back.

"We can do the whole kit and caboodle for ya," said Dilly. "That's what doodles are for. If you've wasted time, we'll find more. If a teacher says, 'Get busy,' we'll go get him for you."

"Doodles are a kid's best friend, Andrew," said Dally. "All doodles except cousin Graffiti. He can get you in big trouble."

Andrew shuffled the papers and workbooks on his desktop. "Well, Dilly-Dally, I have a ton of work to do," he said. "I guess I could use some help."

"Then hand me some pencils, mate," said Dilly.

"And let the doodles do your work," said Dally. Andrew took a pencil box from his desk. He put a pencil in each of Dilly-Dally's hands. At once the beast began plodding around the math paper, filling in answers.

"I hope you're good at math," said Andrew. "If an answer is wrong, the teacher makes me do the problem all over again."

"Don't worry, mate, we always use our doodle noodles," said Dilly.

"But this work would get done much faster if you drew more doodles to help us out," Dally added.

Andrew picked up his pencil. "More doodles?" he said. "Sure, I can do that."

He drew a rooster at the bottom of the handwriting sheet. Instantly the bird sprouted from the paper, calling, "Cock-a-doodle-dooooo!"

Andrew handed the rooster a pencil and watched it write a neat row of capital *Q*'s. Nodding in approval, he regarded his story paper.

"Dilly-Dally, can doodles write stories?" he asked. "I sure would like to get caught up on this work by the end of recess."

"Doodles'll do it all for ya, mate," said Dilly.

"Draw oodles of doodles, Andrew," Dally added.

At the top of the story paper, Andrew drew a heart and a smiley face. He added arms and legs to both. Sure enough, the figures popped out of the paper, and after Andrew handed them a pencil, they began waddling along the blue lines, composing a story.

Andrew leaned back in his chair, his hands behind his head. "This is more like it," he said. "I'll have my work completed in no time."

Five minutes later he checked the doodles' progress.

"Math ... done. Spelling and handwriting ... all finished. And my story is long enough. OK, Dilly-Dally, you and the other doodles can quit working now."

The creature, however, ignored Andrew. Rather

than stopping, it flipped the math sheet over and began doing more multiplication problems.

Andrew tapped his pencil on the desktop. "That's enough, Dilly-Dally!" he said. "You're doing tomorrow's math. The teacher gets mad when we work ahead."

"These problems are no problem for us, mate," said Dilly.

"A doodle's work is never done," said Dally.

In the meantime, the other doodles had leaped off Andrew's desk. They landed on Kate's desktop and began completing answers in her spelling workbook.

Andrew's eyes widened. "Hey, stop!" he cried out. "What are you doodles doing? Don't do that. Get off of there!"

He rechecked the clock. In four minutes the playground bell would ring.

"What will the teacher think when he comes back?" Andrew asked himself. "He'll know I had help! I gotta get rid of these doodles!"

To make matters worse, each doodle now started drawing its own doodles. In turn, a doodle robot and a doodle rabbit rose from Kate's spelling book. "Hoo! Hoo!" went a doodle owl that appeared shortly afterward. A doodle dragon breathing doodle fire popped up next. Each doodle grabbed a pencil, jumped to another desktop, and started working.

Andrew got to his feet. He raced around the room waving his pencil as if conducting a band. "Stop, doodles! Don't do that! You doodles skedaddle!"

On Morgan's desk a doodle octopus completed a crossword puzzle. On George's desk a doodle poodle finished writing a limerick.

"Singing polly wolly doodle all the day," sang a doodle parrot, flying onto the reading table.

A doodle dinosaur, angel, and teddy bear appeared. Each doodle drew more doodles that drew more doodles. By now every desktop in the classroom had doodles swarming all over it.

"What can I do about all these doodles?" asked Andrew.

"Toot! Tooooot!" went a doodle train circling his feet.

A monkey on a skateboard scooted by, shouting, "Yahooo!"

At that moment Andrew's luck changed. As he waved his pencil in front of him, the eraser brushed up against a doodle snowman on Hari's desk. Wherever the eraser touched, the doodle disappeared. There stood a snowman with a top and bottom, but minus a middle.

"That's it!" Andrew exclaimed. "That's how to get rid of these doodles! I can erase them as if they were still on paper!" He reached inside his desk for a large pink eraser. "So now it's time for *me* to get to work. Doodles, prepare to do battle!"

As if engaged in a lively sword fight, Andrew swept around the room brandishing his eraser. On Mimi's desk he erased a dancing tin can. He rubbed out a pig with wings that was flying past his nose. He erased a doodle pumpkin and pair of lips roaming round Richard's desk. Away went a doodle walrus wearing a top hat and a doodle duck swimming in the sink.

"So long, sucker," Andrew snarled as he erased a doodle anteater.

"Cock-a-doodle-dooooo," crowed the rooster, and it too disappeared.

Next Andrew pounced on a bounding doodle kangaroo. He dodged doodle arrows to erase a doodle Cupid and chased the doodle poodle into the coat closet. When he had it cornered, the poodle did a doodle piddle before he could wipe it away.

Breathing hard, Andrew checked the clock. "One minute until the bell," he said. "But I have more work to do." He hastened from desk to desk, erasing any evidence that a doodle had been there.

Finally only Dilly-Dally remained. The beast

was still on Andrew's desk, filling in math answers and whistling "Yankee Doodle."

As Andrew approached, Dilly shook its head. "Ya wasted some good doodles there, mate," it said.

Dally nodded and added, "But if you ever need any of us again, just pick up a pencil and doodle."

Andrew sat down exhausted. "No thanks," he said, raising his eraser. "Toodle-oo, doodle." And the creature was gone.

When the tall teacher returned to the room he headed straight to Andrew's desk. He looked at the papers and workbooks and nodded.

"Andrew, you really applied yourself during recess," he said. "All your work is completed. I also see that you erased those doodles. Good for you." Then the teacher walked up to the blackboard to write the next assignment.

Andrew blew out his cheeks. "Schoolwork," he grumbled. "As soon as you get done with one assignment, another one comes along."

He started doodling a rattlesnake on the back of a workbook when he caught himself. He looked up at the blackboard.

"So maybe I'll just start working on it. I'd hate to fall behind."

The Chatterbox

Morgan turned in her seat. "Did you know it's impossible to sneeze with your eyes open?" she said to Danny behind her. "Last night I kept sneezing, and my eyes shut every time. Weird. They just shut."

Danny stared at his worksheet, trying to remember the difference between a synonym and an antonym. "Quiet, Morgan!" he snarled. "Turn around! Stop bugging me!"

Morgan leaned forward and peered over Kate's shoulder. "Did you know there's only one spot in the United States where four states touch?" she said. "Colorado, New Mexico, Arizona, and Utah. I checked a map last night. Weird. That's the only spot where four states come together."

"Shhhhh," hissed Kate. "Leave me alone."

Morgan turned left to tell Gabrielle why stars twinkle at night and planets don't. Then she turned right to tell Hari about the car painted with zebra stripes that she spotted on the way to school. Each time she received the same shushes and sour looks. She ended up talking to her desktop. "Why doesn't anyone want to talk to me? No one even likes me."

In the front of the classroom the tall teacher sat behind his large metal desk. He looked up at the clock above the green blackboard and announced, "Lunchtime, class. Let's get our lunches and make a straight line at the door."

Swoosh! The third-graders rushed to the coat closet, grabbed their lunchboxes, and formed a Z-shaped line at the door.

Morgan stood behind Richard. "Did you know there once was a lady who ate chicken at every meal, and she died?" she told him. "That's the only thing she ever ate, chicken. I guess she didn't get enough vitamins and minerals and stuff, so she died."

Morgan turned around and said to George, "Have you noticed that the teacher's ears turn red whenever he gets mad? Weird. You can always tell when he's mad because his ears turn red."

"Motormouth Morgan. Gab, gab, gab. Yakety-yak-

yak. Blah, blah, blah," her classmates said as they filed from the room. But Morgan didn't hear them. She was too busy chatting.

The gym at W. T. Melon Elementary School served as the P.E. room, the assembly room, and the room where classes put on plays. Now tables and benches stuck out from the walls and the gym became the lunchroom, complete with flying straw wrappers, popping sandwich bags, and the smell of spaghetti.

Morgan sat at the third-grade table next to Kate and Mimi. "Did you know a hard-boiled egg will explode in a microwave oven?" she said. "Last night I proved it. Pow! The egg blew up all right, and I had to spend my entire TV time scrubbing the inside of our microwave."

Scooch, scooch, scooch. Kate and Mimi slid down the bench.

Left alone, Morgan looked toward the two girls. "No one wants to talk with me," she repeated. "No one even likes me."

Finally Morgan turned her attention to lunch. For the first time she noticed something different about her lunchbox. The red plastic box plastered with stickers was the same one she carried every day to school. But now on the lid, printed in silver glitter, were two words:

MORGAN'S CHATTERBOX

"Weird," Morgan muttered.

She flipped the latch and opened the lid. Inside, next to a baloney sandwich and a hard-boiled egg, she found a calculator. Underneath was a card that read:

Win! Win! Win!
Play the Chatterbox Game!
Fabulous Prize!
Say under 100 words today, and you're the winner!

For once Morgan was speechless. She inspected the calculator and pushed the ON button. Nothing happened.

"Busted," she muttered.

As she spoke, however, a **1** appeared on the liquid-crystal display.

"Weird."

And a **2** appeared.

"Real weird."

3 ... 4

"It's counting my words," she said.

5 ... 6 ... 7 ... 8

"Hello? Hello?"

9 ... 10

Morgan reread the card. Now I know how to play the Chatterbox Game, she said in her head, careful not to speak out loud. This calculator counts my words. Again she checked the card. If I say fewer than one hundred words, I'll win a prize. Cinch! One hundred words are a lot of words.

"It's a deal, Chatterbox," she said to her lunchbox.

11 ... 12 ... 13 ... 14

Morgan slapped her hand over her mouth. Two and a half hours remained before school was out. She wouldn't waste one more word.

Back in the classroom Morgan placed the calculator in the pencil groove on her desktop. She ran pinched fingers across her lips to show they were zipped shut.

Up front the tall teacher held a twig with a crinkled gray sack attached. "This is a cocoon, class," he said. "For science today we'll talk about the life cycle of the butterfly."

From the fourth row came a voice. "Caterpillars spin cocoons. I find caterpillars all the time in my backyard. They look like little mustaches crawling on leaves. I once saw a boy eat a caterpillar. Weird."

Morgan was at it again. She prattled on about caterpillars until the teacher, his ears glowing red, cut her off with a sharp "Thank you, Morgan."

Morgan's jaws snapped shut. She stared at the **90** on the calculator display. "Only ten words left," she said.

91 ... 92 ... 93 ... 94

"Geez," Morgan muttered.

95

"Hey, that's not a word."

100 ... 100 ... 100 ... flashed the screen before going blank.

Morgan frowned. "Oh, well, I lost the Chatterbox Game," she told herself. "But at least I got to tell the class what I know about caterpillars."

The next morning the Chatterbox was far from Morgan's mind as she walked to school. She swung her lunchbox in her hand. At the corner she met Mimi and Kate.

"Did you know there are no words that rhyme with orange?" she told them. "Porange? Gorange? Morange? Nope. There's not one word that rhymes with orange."

The crossing guard held up her stop sign. The moment she stepped into the yellow crosswalk, Mimi and Kate hurried across the street.

Morgan crossed alone. "No one wants to talk with

me," she said again. "Why doesn't anyone like me?"

As she continued on to school, Morgan thought about the things she would tell her classmates that morning. She was crossing the playground when something peculiar happened. Her lunchbox began to vibrate, sending shivers up her arm. She held the box to her ear. From inside came a buzz, the sound of a hundred people chattering at once.

Morgan turned the lunchbox around. More silver words appeared on the lid:

MORGAN'S CHATTERBOX II

"Maybe, just maybe, there'll be another game today!" she said to herself.

She opened the lid. This time, a digital watch with a blank face lay next to her baloney sandwich. Another card read:

Win! Win!
Play the Chatterbox Game Again!
Say under 100 words, and win a prize!

"Testing," Morgan said to the watch. When a **l** appeared on the screen, she twisted her fingers on her lips to lock them shut. Not another word would come out of her mouth for the rest of the day.

That morning Morgan had no trouble keeping quiet.

"Would you like to clean the chalk erasers,

Morgan?" the tall teacher asked after taking attendance.

Morgan nodded.

"How much is eighteen divided by six?" Danny asked during math.

Morgan held up three fingers.

"What's the homework assignment for tonight?" Hari asked before recess.

And Morgan shrugged.

On the playground, however, Richard dumped sand down Morgan's back.

"You creep! Pick on someone your own size," she shouted. "Oh, I forgot, you're so fat, no one else is your size." That used twenty words, but she felt much better after saying them.

At lunchtime the watch showed **34**. Even when Mimi and Kate sat by her, Morgan kept quiet and listened.

"I'll win the Chatterbox Game today for sure," she told herself back in the classroom. "Mum's the word."

The tall teacher held up a jar. "This afternoon, class, we'll examine pillbugs," he said. "Does anyone know why we call these pillbugs?"

Morgan wriggled in her seat. Oh, how she wanted to answer! She was a pillbug expert. She could speak for an hour about pillbugs. She bit her tongue. She pounded her desktop with her fist. Finally her mouth burst open.

"Because they roll into a little pill if you touch them!" she blurted out.

Numbers blinked on the watch.

"Some people call them roly-polies," Morgan jabbered on. "I find roly-polies under rocks all the time. I have roly-poly races, and I once made a roly-poly village. I kept the village in a box under my bed, but my cat tipped it over, and my mom had a fit."

The watch flashed **100** ... **100** ... **100**.

Morgan sighed. "This Chatterbox Game is harder to win than I thought."

The next morning it happened again. As Morgan walked across the playground, her lunchbox quivered in her hand. The babbling of voices came from within, and more silver words appeared on the lid:

MORGAN'S CHATTERBOX III

This time she found a hand-held video game lying next to her baloney sandwich. Another card read:

Last chance!
You can be a winner!
Remember, under 100 words!
A spectacular prize awaits you!

Today that Chatterbox wouldn't hear a peep out of her, Morgan decided. The cat would get her tongue, and she'd be as quiet as a mouse. With her lips squeezed tight, she marched up the school steps.

That morning Mimi asked Morgan if she could borrow a pencil.

"Sure," Morgan replied, and a **1** appeared on the video game screen.

Later Danny said to Morgan, "I found this cool set of teeth on my grandpa's nightstand. So I brought it in for Show and Tell."

"Weird," Morgan said, and the screen showed **2**.

At lunch Mimi demonstrated to Morgan how to make milk come out of her nose, and Kate told her about the time she ate poison ivy. "Yuck! Cool! Really?" was all Morgan said.

At one o'clock the video game screen read only **7**. "Today the Chatterbox Game prize is mine," she said to herself.

At the front of the room the tall teacher held up a shoebox. "In here are tiny silkworms," he said. "For the next two weeks we'll feed them mulberry leaves and watch them grow."

Throughout the lesson Morgan listened. To her surprise, she even learned something new about silkworms. When the bell rang at the end of the day she checked the game screen. It flashed:

WINNER! WINNER! WINNER!

"I did it!" Morgan said aloud. But she didn't search for the prize. Somehow she already knew what it was. When she fetched her lunchbox from the coat closet, she noticed that the silver glitter had vanished. Inside, she found only her half-eaten baloney sandwich.

"Morgan, come walk home with us," Mimi called to her.

"If you step on a sidewalk crack you must kiss the cement," said Kate.

Morgan nodded. She closed her lunchbox and followed the girls out the door.

The Playground Court

Each recess the Playground Lady stood in the exact center of the playground. She was a wide, solidly packed woman with squinty eyes and round red cheeks. Her arms remained clasped behind her, and a silver whistle was always plugged between her thick wet lips.

This whistle was no ordinary whistle. It was the one known throughout W. T. Melon Elementary School as the Bad-News Whistle. Any student who heard it knew bad news soon followed.

Treeeeeeeeep! the Bad-News Whistle would blast. "Don't kick the red balls!" the Playground Lady shouted. "Don't stand on the swing! Don't throw sand!"

Treeeeeeeeep! "Keep off the fence! Keep out of the mud! Keep your hands to yourselves!" she bellowed.

Treeeeeeeeeep! "Share the jump ropes. Share the tetherball! Share the tire swing!"

No one liked to hear the Bad-News Whistle blow.

The person for whom the Bad-News Whistle blew the most was a third-grader named Richard. Richard was the terror of the W. T. Melon playground. Every recess he would charge out of the school and climb straight to the top of the jungle gym. Shaking a beefy arm in the air, he would announce, "I'm the King of the Playground. And anyone who doesn't know it, prepare for punishment."

Soon the Bad-News Whistle would start to blow.

Treeeeeeeeeep! "Richard! Give Sherwood back his shirt!"

Treeeeeeeeeep! "Richard, untie Pamela's pigtails from the fence."

Treeeeeeeeeep! Treeeeeeeeeep! Treeeeeeeeeep! The Playground Lady wore herself out blowing her whistle at Richard.

But one morning at recess this all changed. The recess started in the usual joyous, noisy way. The third-graders charged to the soccer field, the second-graders raced for the four-square courts, and the first-graders headed toward the equipment area.

Richard, the lone third-grader not on the grass, took his position at the top of the jungle gym.

"I am the King of the Playground," he proclaimed. "And anyone who doesn't know it, prepare for punishment." Then he scanned the playground for his first victim.

Near a tetherball pole a first-grade girl was jumping rope. Rung by rung, Richard climbed down the jungle gym to the rubber mat and approached her. "Who's the King of the Playground?" he asked.

The girl's eyes grew wide with terror. Her chin quivered as she peeped, "The principal? My teacher?"

"Guess again, peewee," said Richard.

The little girl trembled so hard her pigtails wobbled like noodles. "The president?" she squeaked. "God, maybe?"

"*Wrong!*" said Richard. "I am King of the Playground." And he tied the girl to the tetherball pole with her jump rope.

Next he stomped up to a first-grade boy climbing the slide ladder. "Who's the King of the Playground?" Richard growled.

The boy gripped the ladder tightly. "I-I-I don't know," he stuttered. "I-I-I don't know."

"That's too bad, runt," said Richard. And he pulled the little boy's pants down to his knees. There he stood shivering, his white underpants gleaming in the morning sun.

"Ha, ha, haaaa!" Richard howled. "*I* am King of the Playground. *I am. I am.*"

For the next ten minutes Richard prowled the playground proving his might. He tied the swing chains in knots so no one could swing. He snatched a red ball from the four-square court and tossed it on the roof. He stomped to the bicycle stand and knocked over the row of bikes. Then he grabbed the smallest first-grader by the ankles and shook him upside down until his lunch money fell from his pockets.

"Who's the King of the Playground?" the bully demanded.

"Yoo-o-o ar-r-r," said the boy. "Yoo-o-o ar-r-r-r."

Richard tramped into the sandbox looking for more trouble. A brave girl looked up from her sand tunnel. "You're mean, Richard," she said. "You should follow the playground rules. That's what they're for."

Richard flattened the girl's tunnel. "Playground rules aren't for me, squirt. I rule the playground." *Treeeeeeeeeep!* When the Bad-News Whistle blew this time, it was for the worst news of all.

"Recess is over!" shouted the Playground Lady. "Let's get back to work!"

The students charged into the school as they had

charged out of it—all but Richard. Never one to hurry back to class, he returned to his perch at the top of the jungle gym. He wished to be the last one off the playground.

But the instant Richard was alone, a tremendous *Bang! Bang! Bang!* shook the playground. One end of the teeter-totter had raised and lowered itself three times, striking the asphalt like a hammer.

What happened next happened so fast that before Richard knew what was happening he found himself lying on the rubber mat, face first. The jungle gym had wobbled and tossed him off.

He rose to his feet, fists raised. "Who did that? I'll flatten you like a blackboard. I'll beat you into chalk dust." But the only thing there to hit was the jungle gym, standing as black and straight as before.

Bump! Something swatted Richard's bottom. He spun around and saw a swing swaying in the swing set.

"Where are you?" he snarled. "No one touches me and gets away with it."

Richard took two steps backward and tripped over the slide.

"How'd that get here?" he said, rubbing his bottom. "The slide was over there. Now it's here."

This time when Richard rose off the mat, he heard sounds—squeaking, rattling, and scraping like metal against asphalt.

"That's creepy," he said under his breath. "The tetherball is moving closer to the tire swing. The tire

swing is moving closer to the monkey bars and slide.
And they're all moving closer to me."

Squeak! Rattle! Scrape! Closer and closer the
playground equipment came until it surrounded
Richard like players in a dodgeball game.

Richard turned in circles. "Hey, what's going on?
This must be some sort of special effect, like in the
movies. But it all looks so real. Sorry I can't stay to
see more. I must get back to class."

The instant he stepped toward the school—
thunk!—the slide shot out like a boot and kicked

him toward the swing set. There chains from two swings wrapped around him and held him fast.

Richard knelt on the rubber mat like a prisoner in a dungeon. The chains jangled as he tried to free himself.

"Hey, let me go. Let me go," he cried. "No fair. You're bigger than I am."

At that instant, a high, sharp voice called from inside the tire swing. "Hear ye, hear ye! The Playground Court is now in session."

"OK, OK, OK," said an invisible speaker on the four-square court. "Geez, can't I get any rest around here?"

Richard shook his chains some more. "Who's saying those things?" he said. "What Playground Court are you talking about?"

Bang! Bang! Bang! Again the teeter-totter pounded the asphalt.

"The next case is Richard versus The Playground," the tire-swing voice stated. "Judge Jungle Gym presiding."

At this point, the tire swing and tetherball pole slid apart. Walking like a giant beetle, the jungle gym waddled into the circle. The tall black structure towered over Richard. It spoke in a deep voice of authority.

"The playground will now come to order. At this trial I will tolerate no monkeyshines from the monkey bars or back talk from the backstop. Will the prosecution approach the bench?"

"Objection, Your Honor!" cried a wooden bench by the sandbox. "I don't want anyone approaching me!"

The slide moved into the circle. "Your Honor, Richard has been accused of a terrible playground crime—*bullying!*"

"He throws things at little kids instead of throwing them at me," declared the basketball hoop.

"He pushes first-graders when he should be pushing my swings," the swing set sang out.

"He kicks bottoms instead of balls," called a yellow ball by the kickball wall.

Judge Gym turned. "Do any more witnesses wish to take the stand?"

"I don't wish to be taken anywhere, but I *am* a witness," the bicycle stand answered. "I've watched Richard knock little kids off bikes dozens of times."

Loud murmurs and cries of agreement rose from all the playground equipment.

Bang! Bang! Bang!

"Order in the court!" Judge Gym called out.

"I'm innocent. I wasn't doing anything," the four-square court complained. "I was just lying here."

The jungle gym slid closer to Richard. "Young man, you heard the charges. How do you plead?"

"Let me go, let me go," the boy begged.

"What does the defense have to say about these bullying complaints?" asked the judge.

At this point the chain-link fence behind Richard rattled. Out of the bar on the bottom came a high, shaky voice. "Your Honor, de fence says de boy can't help being a bully. He has a defect called Bullying Addiction Disorder, B.A.D. for short. In all my years on de bar I've never defended such a delightful boy. De fence rests its case."

Richard looked toward the sky. "I'm doomed," he muttered.

"The Playground Court will now take a short recess," said Judge Gym. "Will the jury proceed to its box?"

At that moment, twelve balls lying about the asphalt started to bounce. Red rubber balls, yellow balls, tennis balls, basketballs, and white volleyballs

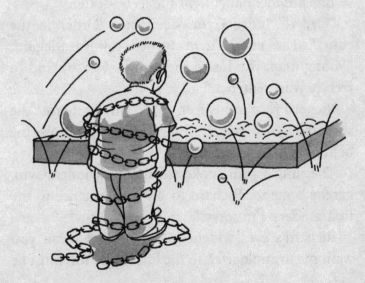

bounded toward the sandbox by the swings. The dozen balls of different colors and sizes lined up on the side of the box facing Richard.

The boy shook his head. "This *must* be some sort of special effect," he said. "Someone must have a remote control close by, making this all happen."

"Ball jury, you have heard the testimony," Judge Gym said. "How do you find Richard?"

Richard stared at the twelve balls. He presented them with his most innocent grin.

The largest red ball rolled forward. "Your Honor," it said, "we the jury find the defendant, Richard, guilty of playground bullying."

Shouts and cheers erupted around the playground. The tire swing spun. The slide rolled up and out like a birthday party noisemaker. Every pole swayed and every bar wobbled.

Bang! Bang! Bang! went the teeter-totter.

"Order!" Judge Gym called out. "Order in the court." The jungle gym turned toward Richard. "Young man, you heard the verdict. Please stand to receive your sentence."

Richard rose to his feet. "My ... my sentence?" he stuttered. "You mean, you're going to throw me behind bars or something?"

The jungle gym spoke solemnly. "I, Judge Gym, hereby sentence Richard to say one sentence to the first-graders: I'm sorry."

Richard's eyes widened. "What? You mean you want me to apologize? To the little kids? You must be kidding. That sentence would be torture."

Squeak! Rattle! Scrape! The tetherball, monkey bars, tire swing, and slide moved closer to Richard.

"OK, OK, I'll say I'm sorry," he said. "Just let me out of here."

"And if you ever start bullying again—" Judge Gym continued.

"—we'll be watching," the rest of the equipment chorused.

"This court is adjourned!" the four-square court announced. "Finally!"

The instant the swings released their hold, Richard peeled across the asphalt toward the school.

"Hang in there, pal," shouted the hanging rings.

"Catch ya next recess, Richard," the basketball hoop called out.

"Monkey see, monkey do," chattered the monkey bars.

"Keep your chin up, Richard," chimed the chin-up bar.

Never had Richard been so glad to be back in the school. He barged into the first-grade classroom and dropped to his knees.

"I'm sorry. Please forgive me, little guys," he begged. "I apologize for everything I've ever done to you at any recess. Let's be pals. My bullying days are over."

The first-graders looked at each other and giggled. Richard did look silly, kneeling there by the teacher's desk.

Miss Hap, the first-grade teacher, smiled. "Richie, I'm so proud of you," she said. Richard returned to the classroom at the end of the hall. During reading he kept peering out the window. If he craned his neck to the left he could see the slide, tire swing, and jungle gym, now standing in their regular spots on the asphalt.

He turned toward Mimi, sitting behind him. "Did you notice anything unusual on the playground after the last recess?" he asked.

"Only you," she replied. "You're sure unusual."

"Just as I thought," Richard said to himself. "There's no such thing as a Playground Court or Judge Jungle Gym. It was all some sort of special effect."

Nevertheless, the following recess and every recess after that, Richard played far away from the equipment area. And not once, for the rest of the school year, did the Bad-News Whistle blow for him.

The Spelling Worm

The class in the room at the end of the hall had been studying insects for three weeks. Butterflies fluttered in a wire cage. Silkworms the size of a teacher's thumb munched mulberry leaves in a plastic tub, and a pickle jar full of pillbugs sat on the science shelf. Even a line of ants paraded past the sink, hauling away cupcake crumbs.

On each desk stood a clear plastic vial. The vials contained three items—an inch of wheat bran, a cube of potato, and a green mealworm.

The tall teacher explained to the class, "Any day now, if you let your worm eat the bran and suck water from the potato, it will change into a white pupa. A week or so after that, it will turn into a brown beetle."

Kate sat in the third row. A label on the side of her vial read, BOB, THE MEALWORM. Her chin rested on her fist as she studied the worm.

"Come on, Bob, change," she said. "You can do it. Don't just be an ugly mealworm.

A mealworm can't do anything but wiggle. Change into a beautiful beetle."

The mealworm squirmed and flipped over twice. But it remained a mealworm.

"Let's get busy, Kate," the tall teacher called out. "You have a story to write. And be careful with your spelling, capitals, punctuation, and handwriting."

Kate stared at the blank sheet of writing paper on her desktop. "Writing stories is a pain, Bob," she said. "Spelling, capitals, punctuation, and handwriting. That's too much to worry about. How can you write a good story with all that on your mind?"

Kate pulled the top off her vial. She dumped the mealworm onto the corner of her desktop.

"My story is supposed to be about an insect, Bob," she said. "So I'll write about you. I'll write how a worthless worm turned into a wonderful beetle."

Copying off her vial, Kate wrote the title: "Bob, the Mealworm." Twenty minutes later, with a jab of her pencil, she added the final period and brought the story up to the teacher's desk.

The tall teacher took one look at the paper and

lost his smile. His expression would have been the same if he'd bitten into a sour apple. "Oh, Kate," he said. "Oh, oh, Kate."

"Are you all right?" Kate asked.

"Your spelling, Kate. You've misspelled almost every word in this story. I can't read what you're trying to say. Please rewrite this entire thing. And if you don't know how to spell a word, use a dictionary."

Kate crumpled the paper and slam-dunked it into the wastebasket. She grabbed another sheet and slunk back to her seat.

"And don't forget to check your capitals, punctuation, and handwriting," the teacher called after her.

Kate rested her chin on her fist and frowned at her worm. "Spelling is the biggest pain of all, Bob," she muttered. "Did you know there are twenty-six letters in the alphabet? How can a kid remember which ones go in which word? And just to confuse us further, some words are spelled in the craziest ways. Did you know there are three ways to spell *to*, Bob? If you ask me, that's two too many ways to spell it. Yes, spelling is impossible."

Again Kate wrote "Bob, the Mealworm" at the top of her paper.

"I'll start my story the way all great stories start: *Once upon a time*," she said. "And from how it sounds, *once* begins with a *w*."

Kate placed her pencil point on her paper. As she began to write, the mealworm wriggled. It flipped over and flipped back again. Finally it curled into a circle the size of a Cheerio.

Kate beamed. "What a coincidence, Bob. You're shaped like an *o*, and *once* begins with an *o*, not a *w*."

The moment she wrote a capital *o* on her paper, the mealworm squirmed again. It stopped, bent in two.

"Now you look like an *n*, Bob," Kate said. "Another coincidence! That's the next letter I need to write."

She wrote down the second letter, and again the worm wriggled. This time it curved like a clipped fingernail.

"Now you're a *c*, Bob," said Kate.

Until this point the girl figured it was a fluke that the mealworm formed letters. After all, mealworms often curl into *o*'s or *n*'s or *c*'s. But when Bob wriggled into the next letter, an *e*, Kate dropped her pencil and her jaw.

"Hey, Bob, what's going on?" she said. "You've spelled the entire word *once*. That's no accident. What's happening here?"

Quickly Kate wrote down the *e* and watched the worm. Yes, it began wriggling again. In quick succession it formed a *u*, a *p*, an *o*, and another *n*.

"Bob, you can spell!" she exclaimed. "And you're spelling the words I need to write my story. I mean, I've heard of a spelling bee, but never a spelling worm."

Again the mealworm went into action. Soon Kate had the entire phrase *Once upon a time* on her paper. Of course, the *t* was tricky for one worm to make. Bob looked more like an upside-down *L*, but Kate knew what shape the worm was trying to curl itself into.

"Mealworms must be smarter than scientists think, Bob," she said. "I bet you pay close attention during our spelling lessons."

Kate wrote the next sentence, the next, and the next. What a relief it was not to worry about spelling! Ideas burst from her brain. Words poured from her pencil. Whenever she forgot how to spell a word, the mealworm curled into the correct letter. No word, not even *people* or *enough*, stumped Bob.

To Kate's great relief, Bob also helped with the punctuation. The worm made excellent exclamation marks and question marks. Its commas and apostrophes were impressive as well.

Twenty minutes later, Kate finished a story two pages long. "Well, I think we stuck in all the right capitals and punctuation marks, Bob," she said, examining the paper. "Handwriting looks good, and won't the teacher be surprised when he sees the spelling."

Proudly she showed the tall teacher her story. Back and forth, back and forth his eyeballs went as he read it. Up and down went his Adam's apple when he turned the page. Finally he said, "Oh, Kate. Oh, oh, Kate."

Kate shuffled her feet. "What's wrong?" she asked. "Did I forgot to do that indenting thing? Did I write an *a* instead of an *an*? I bet I didn't stick enough of those squiggly marks in my conversations."

"No, Kate, this story is terrific," said the teacher. "I never knew you could write such a clever, funny story."

Kate let out a long breath of air. "Neither did I," she said.

The teacher wrote A+++ at the top of the paper. Then he stood and read Kate's story to the class. When he finished everyone clapped.

Smiling and flushed, Kate returned to her seat. "Did you hear that, Bob?" she said to the vial. "They liked my story. No one complained about spelling, capitals, or punctuation. Writing isn't such a pain after all."

For the rest of the week Kate wrote whenever she could. She penciled long passages in her daily journal. She composed page after page of stories. Even in her spare time she grabbed some paper and wrote letters to her grandparents, notes to friends, and poems to no one in particular.

The mealworm kept busy, helping Kate spell any word she didn't know. On Friday, Kate was tempted to watch it during her spelling test. But that, of course, would have been cheating.

"Maybe I'll be a writer when I grow up, Bob," she said. "Maybe I'll write a great book and win the Newbery Award, the Pulitzer Prize, and the Nobel Prize all at once. Maybe I'll even get my name in the W. T. Melon school newspaper."

Monday morning a surprise awaited Kate on her desktop. The mealworm had vanished from the vial. In its place lay a white, comma-shaped blob of jelly.

"Well, look at you, Bob!" she said. "You're no longer Bob the mealworm. Now you're Bob the pupa. This'll make a great story."

She pulled her journal from her desk and wrote in a whirl. Not until the second paragraph did she stop and stare at the pupa. "I need to spell *magic*, Bob. But I guess you can't show me anymore."

She thought a moment before doing something she had rarely done before. She reached into her desk and took out her Webster's dictionary.

"Dictionaries are a pain, Bob," she said. "Before I can find a word in this fat book, I forget what I wanted to write in the first place. Spelling worms are far more handy. But I've learned that people don't like reading stories with lots of misspelled words."

Two weeks later a second miracle occurred on Kate's desk. Now a gleaming brown beetle sat in the plastic vial.

"Congratulations, Bob!" she said. "You're more beautiful than I imagined."

That afternoon the class painted insect pictures. While painting, Kate pulled off the vial cap and let the beetle explore her desktop. Almost at once it crawled through a glob of blue paint. Kate watched it scurry around her paper, writing neat cursive letters. Finally it hopped, printing a blue period at the end of a sentence.

Bye-bye, Kate.
I'm off to another classroom for a spell.

"Bob! Not only can you still spell well, but you have excellent handwriting," Kate said. Then she watched the beetle crawl off her desk, across the floor, up the wall, and out the classroom window.

"So long, Bob," Kate called out, and she picked up her pencil to begin another story.

Throughout the rest of the year Kate wrote many fine stories. Although she never became a great speller, she did remember that people preferred reading her stories if the words were spelled correctly.

Sometimes the tall teacher let Kate write on the computer. Before she printed her stories, she always hit the Spell-Check key. Any misspelled word would flash, flash, flash for her to correct. Kate had a name for that Spell-Check key. She called it Bob.

The Catchiest Tune

 George rocked back in his chair. That raised the front legs three inches off the music room floor.

"George, dear, keep your chair flat on the floor," said Miss Sing, the music teacher. "You could tip over and hurt yourself."

Miss Sing sat behind her piano. George had a view of her high brown hair, round head, and sloping shoulders. He was wondering what the rest of the teacher looked like, when—*slam!*—he fell backward.

"George, dear, are you all right?" Miss Sing called out. "What did I tell you about leaning back in your seat?"

George stood, rubbing his bottom. "Gee!" he exclaimed. "Gee!" He had to endure the gibes and snickers from his classmates as he righted his chair.

Next the music teacher held up a long, thin vinyl

case. "Today, boys and girls, we begin playing the recorder," she said. "When you get your new instrument, leave it in the case until I give further directions."

George was delighted. Ever since first grade he had dreamed of playing the recorder. Every year he listened to the third-graders in the music room play "Frère Jacques" and "Lightly Row." Now it was his turn.

After receiving his recorder, George pulled it from the case and blew into the mouthpiece. Out came a squeal like a puppy in pain.

The music teacher looked over her piano. "George, dear," she said. "What did I tell you about playing your instrument?"

For the next half-hour Miss Sing showed the third-graders how to hold a recorder and how to cover the holes with the pads of their fingers. At last she said, "Now, boys and girls, place the mouthpiece between your lips. Don't blow, say 'Tuh-tuh-tuh.' Cover the top three holes, say 'Tuh-tuh-tuh,' and you'll hear a soft G note."

Soon the music room filled with squeaks, squeals, and an occasional G.

"That's all for today, boys and girls," Miss Sing said. "Return your instrument to its case, and you may go to recess. Do not play your recorder on the playground."

But George's recorder remained in his mouth. He marched across the music room playing *G G G* right out the door.

G G G he played down the hall to the playground.

G G G he played as he tramped past the Playground Lady, who wasn't sure whether to blow her whistle or not.

G G G he played from the slide to the monkey bars and back again.

Finally George lowered his recorder. "I think I know G well enough," he said. "Maybe Miss Sing will teach me another note. I want to learn every one of them from A to Z." So George played *G G G* all the way back to the music room.

The room, however, was vacant. He was about to leave when a videotape on top of the piano caught his eye. The label read:

LEARN TO PLAY THE RECORDER
IN ONE E-Z LESSON.

"Just what I need!" George exclaimed. "If I watch this video, maybe I can become the best recorder player in the school."

He took the tape to the VCR in the rear of the room. He pushed the ON button and inserted the tape in the proper slot. After the FBI warning, a fancy room appeared on the screen. Tall windows with golden curtains lined the walls. Crystal chandeliers hung from the ceiling.

In the middle of the room stood a piano. A boy of about twelve sat on a bench playing it. He wore a ruffled shirt and knee breeches not unlike the pants an NFL quarterback might wear. A powdered wig with a short pigtail covered his head.

George was enjoying the piano music when the boy suddenly stopped playing. He stared straight at George. "Hello, George," he said. "That was a piano piece I wrote. It's called Sonata in G."

George was stunned. How could a video be talking to him?

"Sonata in G?" he said. "Why, I can play G on my recorder."

The boy grinned. "So I've heard, George. And you play it very well."

George scuffed the floor with the toe of his sneakers. "But that's all I know so far. And I'm getting tired of it."

"I imagine the whole school is," said the boy. "But now I can be your teacher. And before I begin your lesson, let me introduce myself. My name is Wolfgang."

"Wolfgang?" said George. "What an odd name. Kids must make fun of you with a name like Wolfgang."

"Unfortunately, I'm rarely around children. I spend my time composing music and playing piano for kings and queens."

"Gee," said George. "I can't even play 'Twinkle, Twinkle, Little Star' on my recorder."

Wolfgang nodded. "Ah, yes, 'Twinkle, Twinkle, Little Star.' That's a tune I play often." He played the melody on his piano, first slowly, then quickly with a bouncy beat.

George snapped his fingers and tapped his toes. "That's very catchy," he said. "It makes me want to dance. A tune like that can get stuck in my head for hours."

"Yes, it can," said Wolfgang. "So imagine what would happen if you heard the Catchiest Tune."

"The Catchiest Tune?" George asked.

"A perfect melody. A tune so catchy you can *never* get it out of your head."

"Gee, that would be something," said George. "But there couldn't be such a thing as the Catchiest Tune, could there?"

"Indeed there could, and I am the composer who composed it," said Wolfgang. "One evening as I was playing a minuet on my piano, the melody popped into my head. I knew at once it was the perfect tune. Believe it or not, George, it has only three notes. The first note is G."

"G? That's the note I know," said George. He played *G G G* on his recorder as a reminder. "So maybe, please, could you, would you teach me the other two notes?"

Wolfgang played some scales on his keyboard. "Well, I don't know, George," he said. "Playing the Catchiest Tune could be dangerous."

"Oh, come on, Wolfgang. If I could play the catchiest song in the world I'd never need to learn any other."

The boy drew a wooden recorder from his pocket. "I'll teach you my tune on one condition," he said.

"I'll do whatever you say," George promised.

"You must follow my directions exactly."

"No problem," said George.

Here Wolfgang pulled two tufts from his powdered wig. He stuffed them into his ears. "I will teach you how to play the Catchiest Tune if you promise never to listen to it," he said. "You must plug your ears as I do whenever you play it. Agreed?"

"Gee. Agreed."

"Then block your ears and watch my fingers," said Wolfgang. "Copy what I do."

George pulled a Kleenex from a box on the reading table. He wedged half a tissue into each ear and returned to the video. He had no problem following Wolfgang's fingers as they moved on and off the holes of his recorder.

"That's it?" said George after a minute of practice. "That's the whole song? But it's so simple." With his ears blocked, his voice sounded loud and hollow. He removed the Kleenex to hear Wolfgang's reply.

"Some of the greatest works of art are the simplest, George. Now you must excuse me. The king is waiting for my concert. But before we part, I must ask again. Are you sure you'll follow my directions about the Catchiest Tune? If you play it, you must never hear it."

George nodded and restuffed his ears. By the time THE END appeared on the video screen, he was already out the music room door.

Back on the playground, George stood by the jungle gym. He held up his recorder. "Ladies and gentlemen, I wish to play a song for you," he announced.

"Here, live on our playground, is the W. T. Melon Elementary School premiere of the Catchiest Tune."

After checking that the tissue wads were firmly in place, George raised the instrument to his lips. "Tuh-tuh-tuh," he said. Up and down went his fingers as Wolfgang had shown him. "Tuh-tuh-tuh. Tuh-tuh-tuh."

The result was instant. The result was astonishing. All movement on the playground—the chasing, running, swinging, and sliding—suddenly ceased. As if in a trance, everyone from the first-graders to the Playground Lady stared at George.

George pointed his recorder toward the sky and played the tune again. His audience starting tapping their toes and bobbing their heads. They all snapped their fingers and flapped their elbows like chickens. When George played the tune a third time, the dancing began.

Some third-graders playing dodgeball waltzed in a circle. First-graders by the swings did the Mexican Hat Dance. Second-graders at the four-square court square-danced, while others leaped and twirled around a tetherball pole like ballet dancers. Even the Playground Lady did an odd sort of twist, leaning far back and twirling her silver whistle around her finger.

Look at everyone go, thought George. Wolfgang

was right. This song must be the catchiest one ever written. And he played the tune again.

Now Mr. Principle, the school principal, and Miss Take, the secretary, walked onto the playground. The instant they heard George's music they faced each other and began doing the cha-cha by the flagpole. Two teachers in the Teachers' Lounge tap-danced, while Miss Sing, listening from the doorway, did the hula-hula.

As George played he had a thought. How come everyone gets to enjoy the music but me? Sure, Wolfgang told me not to hear it, but teachers are always making up silly rules. They say don't wear a coat in the classroom, but I still wear mine. What happens? Nothing. They say never chew gum at school, but I still chew some. What goes wrong? Nothing. No, teachers give directions just to be teachers. What could happen if I heard Wolfgang's song? Not a thing.

George lowered his recorder and pulled the Kleenex from his ears.

"Play it again, George! Let her

rip!" the people on the playground called to him. "Come on, George, blow that thing!"

George returned the recorder to his lips and said, "Tuh-tuh-tuh." This time he heard the G. He heard the next note and the next note as well. Gee, this song is catchy, he thought. And he started doing a quick jig right there by the slide.

He played the song some more and he jigged some more. He played and jigged around the jungle gym. He played and jigged in and out of the swing set. He played and jigged from one basketball hoop to the other.

Meanwhile, the fourth grade filed from the school in a long conga line. The fifth grade came out doing the bunny hop. By now the playground was a mass of teachers and students dancing the can-can, the rumba, the fox-trot, the funky chicken, the tango, and a Native American rain dance. A circle of teachers stood by the bicycle rack doing the hokey-pokey.

All this time, as George played, he jigged. By now his legs were weary. His fingers ached and his lips were numb from saying "Tuh-tuh-tuh" so many times.

"OK, that's enough," he told himself. "Time to stop the music."

To his surprise, however, he repeated the Catchiest Tune anyway and went on jigging.

"Now I really must stop this song," George said in his head. "My legs are ready to fall off their hinges. The bottoms of my sneakers must be worn right through."

But he still played, and he still jigged.

That was when George realized something dreadful. He couldn't lower his recorder. He couldn't stop saying, "Tuh-tuh-tuh." He was hooked. The tune was so catchy he had to hear it over and over. Even worse, since he couldn't stop playing the Catchiest Tune, he couldn't stop jigging.

Shivers swept up George's spine as he jigged toward the baseball diamond. Would he keep dancing for the rest of the day? he wondered. For the rest of the year? He didn't think he could jig one more minute.

Kicking up dust, he jigged from second to third base. Oh, how his legs suffered. His feet were on fire. He jigged to home plate, on to first, and back to second. *Help! Help!* he wanted to call out. But he couldn't. He could only repeat the tune for the twentieth time.

Fortunately, at that moment Mr. Leeks, the school janitor, came riding around the corner of the school on his lawn mower. He was planning to mow the soccer field. The mower was noisy, so he couldn't hear George's tune. Mr. Leeks had been working at W. T. Melon a long time and had seen many strange things. So when he saw George playing his recorder and the entire student body and staff dancing, he knew better than to turn off the lawn mower.

Cranking the throttle up full speed, the janitor directed the lawn mower toward the baseball diamond. "Charge!" he cried.

Like a knight on a steed, he raced toward George as he jigged around the bases. Without stopping, Mr. Leeks reached out and snatched the recorder from his hands.

George instantly stopped dancing. He dropped to his knees, breathing hard. "Gee," he sputtered.

Across the playground the twisting, fox-trotting, and belly-dancing stopped as well.

"What in tarnation is going on here?" Mr. Leeks called to George.

George rubbed his feet. "I-I was just playing my recorder," he said. "And this boy Wolfgang on a video taught me a catchy tune."

Mr. Leeks kneaded his scratchy chin. "Just playing your recorder, eh?" he said. "Taught you a tune, eh?"

"Wolfgang told me never to listen to the tune if I

played it," George went on. "And I guess I didn't follow directions."

The janitor, who knew George well, handed back the recorder. "Same old song and dance, eh, George?" he said. Then he revved up his lawn mower and sped toward the grass.

At that moment the end-of-recess bell rang. As if nothing out of the ordinary had happened, the students and staff headed for the school doors.

George ran toward the school. He entered the hallway at a full trot.

"Walk in the hall, George," the Playground Lady called out.

George peered toward his classroom at the end of the hall. "What could possibly go wrong if I ran?" he asked himself. But he didn't run. He followed directions and walked all the way.

The Pencil Loser

"Please take out a pencil and paper, class," the tall teacher called out. "Time to practice our cursive handwriting."

In the back row by the window, Mimi opened her desk. She took out a yellow pencil pitted with nibble marks. She cocked the paper on her desktop to the correct handwriting angle. She planted her feet flat on the floor and placed her left arm in the correct handwriting position. Finally she stuck the pencil in her kneesock where it would be easy to reach when she needed to write.

The teacher leaned against the blackboard. "Today we will write tall loops, class," he said. "The cursive letters f and k have tall loops, and a tall loop by itself is an *l*." His hand swooped up, down, up, down, writing a row of tall loops across the blackboard. "Now you try. Write three lines of tall loops. Remember to use the correct handwriting posture and correct pencil grip."

"This looks like fun," said Mimi. "Cursive writing is a lot like doodling."

She bent her back slightly. Her shoulders faced the desk squarely. She was now ready to write, except for one thing.

"Where's my pencil?" she said. "What happened to that thing?"

She checked the groove at the top of her desktop. Empty. She checked her shirt pocket and the pockets of her skirt. Not there either. She looked under her desk and under her neighbors' desks.

"It just disappeared," she said. "It vanished into thin air."

Her arm shot up as stiff and straight as a flagpole. "I can't find my pencil," she called out. "Could I borrow one?"

The teacher leaned on the blackboard again, smearing the tall loops he had just written. His ears were red. "Mimi, that is the umpteenth pencil you lost today," he said. "This is the umpteenth pencil I must lend you. You lost a pencil during math. You lost a pencil before spelling and when you went to the girls' room. You lost a pencil when you went to sharpen it at the sharpener. What's happening to all your pencils?"

Mimi shrugged. She had learned that it's hard for a teacher to argue against a shrug.

The tall teacher drew a new yellow pencil from his desk drawer. "This is the last one, Mimi," he said. "You must stop losing your pencils. Understand?"

Wearing the most innocent look she had, Mimi took the pencil. She trudged to the sharpener screwed to the windowsill by her desk. She crammed it into the hole marked STANDARD and turned the crank.

"It's not my fault," she said. "My pencils just disappear." *Krrrrr! Krrrrr! Krrrrr!* went the sharpener. "They vanish into thin air."

Mimi pulled out the pencil and blew on the tip. Having had so much practice, she put on a perfect point every time. She set the pencil on the windowsill and watched Mr. Leeks mow the soccer field before taking her seat.

Again she placed her feet flat on the floor. Again she bent her back and laid her left arm across the top of the paper. And again she said, "Where's my pencil?"

The groove on her desktop was empty. Her pocket held nothing, and the only thing under her desk was a mealworm beetle crawling toward a cookie crumb.

"Now what?" she said. "I can't ask the teacher for another pencil until he cools down a bit. My tall loops will never get done."

Mimi had her head buried in her desk, searching for another pencil, when—*Krrrrr! Krrrrr! Krrrrr!*—the sharpener began to grind.

"How could that be?" she asked herself. "No one passed my desk."

She sat up straight and looked toward the window. What she saw at the sharpener was so curious she didn't know whether to laugh or to shout. The thing—one could hardly call it a creature—was as tall as a pencil and as thin as a pencil. It had a six-sided, banana-yellow body like a pencil. Its pointed head and pink boots resembled  the top and bottom of a pencil as well. Mimi would have sworn it *was* a pencil if it didn't stand on two wiry legs and turn the sharpener crank with two wiry arms.

The pencil in the sharpener grew shorter and shorter. When it disappeared altogether, the thing unsnapped the shavings holder and emptied the contents into a sack by its side.

Finally Mimi found her voice. "Hey you, that was *my* pencil you just ground up," she called out. "I needed it to write tall loops."

The short, thin, pointy yellow thing turned toward her. A smile spread across its face, almost doubling its narrow width. "Too bad, little girl," it said. "I find, I grind."

Mimi scowled. "Who are you? What are you? And I'm not a little girl."

The thing stood up straight. "Surely you've heard of me. My name is written on the side of many pencils. I'm Ticonderoga 2, the Pencil Grinder. But you can call me Ti-2, little girl."

"Well, Ti-2," Mimi said. "Just what are you doing in my classroom? And why did you grind up my pencil? And I'm *not* a little girl."

The thing pulled a candy-cane-striped pencil from behind the globe. It inserted it into the sharpener and resumed grinding. "What the Pencil Grinder finds, it grinds," it repeated. "And thanks to you, little girl, this classroom is a bonanza for lost pencils. I find them all over this place—inside books, behind the aquarium, in the wastebasket, under chairs, up in the lights, and stuck in chalk erasers."

"But why grind them up?" Mimi asked. "What good are pencil shavings?"

"Once I sort them, shavings are worth their weight in gold," the thing replied. "The lower-grade shavings I sell to playground makers who press them flat with giant steamrollers. That's how the surfaces of school playgrounds are made. But the choicest shavings I sell to the great chefs of Pennsylvania."

"The chefs of Pennsylvania!" Mimi exclaimed. "Whatever for?"

Ti-2 kissed the ends of his fingers. "The chefs of Pennsylvania use my Grade-A shavings in their exquisite cuisine, little girl. Mmmm-mm. Ever have pencil-shaving stew? Deeeeelicious. Pencil shavings and pasta? Deeeeelectable. Or have you tried the favorite drink of Pennsylvanians, pencil-shaving tea? Deeeeelightful."

Mimi wrinkled her nose and said, "Whatever."

Having ground up the candy-cane-striped pencil, Ti-2 again unloaded the shavings into his sack. Next, the thing stuck a yellow pencil pocked with nibble marks in the sharpener.

"And look at this beauty I found inside a kneesock," it said. "The chefs of Pennsylvania can make pencil-shaving cupcakes, enough birthday treats for an entire class, after I grind this baby up."

Mimi stood and snatched the pencil out of the hole. "That's another of *my* pencils, thank you very much," she said. "Now go away, Pencil Grinder. I have rows of loopy *l*'s to write."

"Don't get cranky, little girl," Ti-2 said. "I'm just doing my job. Kids grow taller and pencils grow shorter. That's a fact of life. But now that I'm fresh out of pencils I think I'll take a nap. Tomorrow I'll get back to the old grind. By then there'll be lots more lost pencils around the classroom for me to find and grind. Nighty-night." With that, the short, thin, pointy yellow thing lay on the windowsill. If Mimi hadn't known better, she would have mistaken it for an ordinary pencil.

First thing the next morning Mimi stood at the pencil sharpener. She put three perfect points on three special pencils. Each one had her name engraved on the side in golden letters.

"Time for cursive handwriting, class," called the tall teacher. "Today we will practice short poles. One short pole makes an *i*, two a *u*, and three a *w*." Up, down, up, down went his hand across the blackboard. "Now it's your turn. Please write three rows of short poles."

Feet flat, back bent, shoulders squared, left hand in position, Mimi reached for her pencil. She was sure she had put it in the desktop groove. But it was gone.

She had barely begun to look for it when—*Krrrrr! Krrrrr!*—the grinding began.

"Good morning, little girl," Ti-2 called from the windowsill. "I found this splendid pencil on the floor. So I thought I'd get the lead out and crank up the sharpener."

Mimi's heart sank. She watched her personalized pencil disappear. "I know, I know," she said through her teeth. "You find, you grind."

She took out a second pencil and started writing short poles. When she finished, she oh-so-carefully placed the pencil in her shirt pocket. Afterward, when she went to P.E., she made sure to put it in the pencil box inside her desk. Unfortunately, during reading she took the pencil to the reading table with her and left it there. In no time—*Krrrrr! Krrrrr!*—Ti-2 was grinding it to shavings.

"They'll be feasting on pencil-shaving pizza tonight in Pennsylvania, little girl," it called out.

Mimi slapped her forehead. "How could I have been so stupid?" she said.

 "What I need is something to remind me not to leave my pencil around the room."

She found a rubber band in her desk and put it on her wrist. Whenever she saw the rubber band she'd think of the pencil. Just to make sure, she stuck a Band-Aid on the back of her hand to remind her what the rubber band was for and wrapped masking tape around her finger to remind her why she wore the Band-Aid.

"I will *not* lose my last pencil," she vowed.

Meanwhile, after emptying the shavings into the sack, Ti-2 hopped off the shelf in search of more pencils. It checked behind the computer, under the butterfly cage, and inside the coat closet.

No one except Mimi seemed to notice the yellow thing. While she watched it scurry around the room, a plan entered her head. She told herself, "Yesterday when the Pencil Grinder ran out of pencils to grind, it took a nap. Maybe if I can keep it from finding more pencils today, it will do the same thing."

At that moment Ti-2 shot toward a pencil by the sink. Mimi lurched from her seat. She pounced on it seconds before the thing got there.

"One less pencil for you, Mr. Ticonderoga," she said. "Perhaps you might be getting a little sleepy with no work to do."

Minutes later, Ti-2 stood on Richard's shoulder. As nimbly as a pickpocket, it was attempting to pinch a pencil from behind his ear.

"Hey, Richard," Mimi called out. "That pencil behind your ear sure looks stupid."

In a flash Richard pulled the pencil out and shook it at Mimi.

She pretended to yawn, irritating both Richard and the thing on his shoulder. "My, wouldn't a nap be nice right now," she said.

Finally, after Mimi had recovered four more pencils, including one left by the tall teacher in the chalk tray, Ti-2 returned to the windowsill. "Poor pencil hunting today, little girl," it called out. "The chefs in Pennsylvania will be disappointed. I guess if I can't grind pencils, I'll saw some logs. Time for a snooze."

Mimi nodded. So far her plan was working. Patiently she watched Ti-2 lie down and close its eyes. She counted to twenty before making her move. In one swift motion she stood, grabbed the yellow thing in her fist, and jammed it into the STAN-DARD hole on the pencil sharpener. It fit perfectly.

Ti-2 woke up grinning. "What do you think you're doing, little girl?" it said. "I'm sharp enough already."

Her jaw set, Mimi turned the crank. *Krrrrr! Krrrrr! Krrrrr!*

The yellow thing giggled. "OK, OK, I think you made your point, little girl. Now get me out of this hole. That grinding tickles."

Krrrrr! Krrrrr! Mimi, with a fierce look in her eye, continued to crank.

"Really, little girl," said Ti-2. "Now I'm only two inches tall. How embarrassing. My friends will call me Stubby. And I have lots of friends, little girl— Ticonderoga 2½, 3, and 4 to name a few. So don't assume that by turning me into shavings you can start being careless with your pencils again. Oh, no, little girl, my friends love looking for lost pencils as much as I do."

At this point only Ti-2's pink boots stuck out of the sharpener. Muttering, Mimi made one last slow turn of the crank. "So long, Leadhead. And ... I'm ... *not* ... a ... little ... girl."

She emptied the shavings not into the wastebasket but into a Baggie in her backpack. After sitting down, she picked up her last engraved pencil. She tapped it on her desktop.

"OK, all you Pencil Grinders, wherever you are," she said. "Just *try* getting this pencil away from me. And as for you, Ticonderoga 2, I'm taking you outside and sprinkling you on the playground. By the end of recess you'll be mashed into the playground surface along with the other low-grade pencil shavings. No, Ti-2, I don't think you're good enough for the chefs of Pennsylvania."

The Fairy Godteacher

Danny was the class complainer. "Do I have to?" he complained whenever the tall teacher called on him and not somebody else. "Not fair! Not faaair!" he complained if the teacher called on somebody else and not him. "This is boooooring," he complained when the schoolwork was too hard. "I know this already," he complained about all other schoolwork.

"She took cuts! I hate this! He got to do it last time! I can't see! His is bigger! Hers was easier! He took cuts! She tripped me! I wanted a blue one! His cupcake has sprinkles and mine doesn't! That's not even! It's not fair! Not faaair!" The way he complained all the time, Danny sounded like the most miserable boy in the world.

One afternoon in the classroom at the end of the hall, the third-graders sat in their seats with books open on their desktops. The room was silent. This period was called S.S.R., which stood for Sustained Silent Reading.

Danny rarely spent S.S.R. time reading. Most often he sat at his desk in the back row, stewing about a problem on the playground the previous recess.

"I got picked last to play soccer," he fumed this time. "Then when I played, everyone started picking on me. It's not faaair!"

Meanwhile, Joey sat in the front row. He was one of the few third-graders who actually read during Sustained Silent Reading time. As he turned a page of his book, a note dropped onto his desktop. On the front it said:

Pass to Danny

Joey turned and gave the note to Andrew, who held it by his side for George to take, and George flipped it to Kate, who dropped it on the floor, allowing Gabrielle to pick it up and hand it to Morgan, who tossed it onto Danny's desk.

Still griping to himself, Danny unfolded the note and read:

Dear Danny,
  Meet me in the library at recess.
    Your Fairy Godteacher

He looked up and scowled. Being in the last row,

he saw the back of every head, but no hint of who sent the note.

"Someone's playing a trick on me, and I hate tricks," he grumbled. "Now I have to wait a whole hour to see what this is all about."

When the recess bell rang, Danny raced straight to the library. Miss Reed, the librarian, stood behind the checkout counter. She held a bar-code scanner that looked remarkably like a pistol. This made Miss Reed appear more like a bank robber than a librarian. She aimed the scanner at the back of a book and zapped it.

"How's school today, Daniel?" she asked.

"Terrible," he groused. "For social studies the teacher talked about boring continents. Then he talked about boring oceans. I never want to live near a continent or an ocean because they all seem boring."

Miss Reed zapped another book. "That's nice, Daniel," she said. "By the way, someone left a note for you on my desk."

This reminded Danny why he had come to the library in the first place. He took the note and read:

Dear Danny,
Meet me in the 398 section.
Your Fairy Godteacher

"What's the 398 section?" Danny asked the librarian.

"Those are the fairy-tale books, Daniel. Halfway down the second aisle."

Danny rushed to the 398 shelves. A third note was sticking out of a book entitled *The Encyclopedia of Fairies*. This one said:

Dear Danny,
  Please open.
    Your Fairy Godteacher

Muttering, "What a waste of time," Danny pulled out the book. He thumbed through pictures of wood fairies, water fairies, sugar-plum fairies, tooth fairies, sprites, pixies, brownies, and fairy godmothers and declared, "Boring!"

Mysteriously, the next page turned by itself. Here Danny saw a picture of a plump, gray-haired fairy the size of a chalk eraser. She wore a floral cotton dress and held a tiny ruler. Wings as clear and thin as a bubble's skin flapped at her shoulders. The caption read: FAIRY GODTEACHER.

"A fairy godteacher?" Danny exclaimed. "I thought it was a joke!"

As he spoke, a fountain of silver glitter shot from the page. Danny held the book out with both hands and closed his eyes. When he reopened them, the very fairy that had been in the picture was hovering five inches in front of his nose.

The fairy shook her ruler at Danny. "Say 'here' when I call your name," she said. "Danny!"

"Huh?" Danny replied.

"No, not 'huh,' young man. Say 'here.'"

"Of course I'm here," said Danny. "Here I am."

The fairy frowned and shook her ruler again. "And don't get snippy with your fairy godteacher, young man."

Danny screwed up his face. "But what *is* a fairy godteacher?"

The fairy bobbed up and down. "Oh, children know so little about fairies nowadays," she said sadly. "Even though every classroom has a fairy godteacher of its own. Even though fairy godteachers have helped countless students whose teachers have treated them unfairly."

Danny nodded. "Teachers are *never* fair to me," he said. "But how could a fairy godteacher help?"

The fairy's wings fluttered faster. She buzzed around Danny's head, stopping before his face again. "Just name your beef, young man, and I have a spell to fix it. Do you hate learning times tables? Well, try my Flash-Through-the-Flash-Cards Spell. When the teacher holds up a flash card, you'll be able to see right through it to the answer on back. Or are you tired of kids cutting in line in front of you? Then try my Cut-the-Cheese Spell. Whoever cuts in front of you gets a strong whiff of rotten cheese. And of course, young man, I've often heard you complain about long spelling lists. But the teacher will assign you only one word a week if I cast my special Spelling Spell."

Danny thought a moment. "But everything in this school seems unfair. They're always out of chocolate milk in the lunch-room. I never get to sit where I want to in music. I can't chew gum. My class never goes on field trips. Only fifth-graders can be on traffic patrol. My reading book has torn pages, and someone always hangs their coat over my coat in the coat closet."

"Sounds like you need a very special spell, young man—my most powerful one," said the fairy godteacher. "Even if your entire life is unfair, this fairy spell will take care of it. What you need, young man, is my all-purpose, heavy-duty, extra-strength Bellyache Spell."

Danny nodded. "That sounds like the spell for

me," he said. "OK, Fairy Godteacher, cast away."

The fairy reached into a pocket. "First, some fairy glitter," she said. Here she tossed a handful of silver glitter onto Danny's nose. "Next, a wave of my wand." And she whipped her ruler in the air as if casting a fishing rod.

Danny inspected his hands and arms. "Your spell didn't work," he complained. "My stomach hurts a little, but that's all."

Before the fairy could answer, the end-of-recess bell rang. "Time for my coffee break, young man," she announced. "I'm off to the Fairy Godteacher Lounge." And with that, she did a swan dive toward *The Encyclopedia of Fairies* and disappeared into its pages.

After recess Danny put on his sneakers for P.E. In the gym he stood along a black line with the rest of his class. They faced Mr. Dumbbell, the P.E. teacher. He was a short, stocky man who wore white sweatpants, a faded blue T-shirt that said W. T. MELON ELEMENTARY SCHOOL on the back, and blue sweatbands around his wrists.

"Third-graders. We'll begin with exercises," Mr. Dumbbell said. "Twenty jumping jacks. Ready?"

Danny folded his arms in front of him. "I hate exercising," he said. "It makes me sweat."

Accustomed to Danny's complaints, the class stood hushed. They waited for the P.E. teacher's reaction. But instead of his usual lecture on the importance of physical fitness, Mr. Dumbbell said

something shocking. "Oh, poor Dan. We don't want you to get all sweaty, do we? We wouldn't think of making you do something you didn't want to."

Danny stepped backwards. Was the teacher making fun of him? No, Mr. Dumbbell was smiling at him without a hint of sarcasm on his face.

"You just stand right there, Dan," the P.E. teacher went on. "Don't worry about doing any of these exercises. Now, all you others. Twenty jumping jacks. Ready? Begin."

Danny's stomach fluttered. He shuffled his feet on the hardwood floor as he watched his classmates do jumping jacks, sit-ups, and deep knee bends. "The fairy godteacher's spell must be working," he told himself. "Finally a teacher is treating me fairly. I exercised twice as hard as anyone last P.E. period. So why shouldn't I get a break this time?"

Afterward, Mr. Dumbbell grinned at Danny. "Good job, Dan," he said. "Now, third-graders, for P.E. today we'll run some relays. And Dan, I know how you hated the relays last week. So you can sit right there for the rest of the period. No, wait. I remember how you disapprove of this dirty floor, so why not go sit on the stage."

"It's only fair," Danny replied as he walked to the stage. "One week I run relays, the next week I rest. Even-steven."

The other third-graders stood with frozen faces. A few muttered words of protest.

After P.E., Miss Count, the computer teacher, stopped the third-graders in the hallway. Danny, at Mr. Dumbbell's urging, was at the head of the line. Miss Count placed a hand on Danny's shoulder and said, "Danny, next time your class comes to the computer lab you can sit at the best computer. I know how you hate the ones with sticky keys."

Farther down the hall Miss Treat, the lunchroom lady, came out of the cafeteria. "Danny, I've heard you fuss about the school's hot lunches. So the cooks are preparing a special lunch just for you, all your favorites—pepperoni pizza, root beer, and a hot fudge sundae."

The pain in Danny's belly sharpened. Grumbles from his classmates followed him down the hall. "This is embarrassing," he said to himself. "But why shouldn't I get what I deserve at school? Teachers have been picking on me for years."

"Yoo-hoo, Danny!" the Playground Lady called from the playground door. "Next recess you get dibs on any ball you want. I'll also make sure you'll never need to whine about anything on the playground again."

"It's Danny's Choice Day in music," Miss Sing sang out from the music room. "We'll sing any song Danny requests."

Danny held his stomach and hurried to his classroom. But when he reached the door, he found Mr. Leeks carrying out his desk and chair.

"Dan, my man!" said the janitor. "I've heard you bellyachin' about the gouges in your desktop for ages. So I've replaced your desk with a spankin' new one. I also brought you a new chair so you won't have to gripe anymore about this old one that squeaks."

Danny blew out his cheeks and turned. His classmates were eyeing him with fury.

Shrugging, he slunk to his new desk in the back row.

When everyone was seated Richard began passing out cupcakes. Today was his birthday.

"Richard," said the tall teacher, "make sure Danny gets the cupcake with the most sprinkles. And remember, he doesn't like chocolate frosting. And since he also doesn't care for the birthday song, we'll skip it today."

Danny slouched farther down in his seat. Richard held a cupcake cocked behind his ear, ready to throw it right at him.

At that moment Mr. Principle's voice came over the intercom. *"Attention, all W. T. Melon students! Due to the unfair treatment Daniel in third grade has been receiving at this school, here are some new school rules. First, since Daniel dislikes the smell in the boys' bathrooms, the one nearest the office will be for his official use only. Second, since Daniel has found that people bump into him in the hallway, all students except Daniel will walk on the left-hand side only. Rule three. Since Daniel is always unable to see the stage during assemblies, there will now be a special tall chair in the front row just for him. Rule four ..."*

As Mr. Principle's voice droned on, a note landed on Danny's desktop. As he suspected, it wasn't from the fairy godteacher. The note read:

Teacher's pet. Teacher's pet.
What Danny wants, he will get.
Your Class Enemies

Danny moaned. "This is unbearable," he said. "The Bellyache Spell has worked so well I doubt I have a friend left in the whole class ... in the whole *school.*" His hand crept upward. "Can I go to the Boys' Room?" he asked. "I gotta go real bad."

The tall teacher smiled. "You can do whatever you want, Danny. Take your time. Stop by the gym and shoot a few baskets, why don't you. Help yourself to the doughnuts in the Teachers' Lounge. If you need a nap, lie down in the nurse's room."

Holding his belly, Danny peeled out the door and straight to the library. He sailed past Miss Reed and hurried to the 398 section.

Upon opening *The Encyclopedia of Fairies*, he said, "OK, Fairy Godteacher, we need to talk."

Silver glitter sprayed from the pages, and the plump fairy appeared before Danny's nose. "Say 'here' when I call your name," she piped out. "Danny!"

"I'm here, and here's what I need," Danny said. "You must take the Bellyache Spell off me. I've become the worst teacher's pet in the school. Kids hate me. *I* don't even like me!"

"But what about all your complaints, young man?" said the fairy. "You said teachers weren't treating you fairly."

"My only complaint is that there's nothing to complain about," said Danny. "I just want teachers to treat me like everyone else. Even-steven."

The fairy buzzed around Danny's head. She whipped her ruler in the air, and the ache in Danny's belly was gone.

"So if you have no further need for me, young man, I'll return to my fairy godteacher's desk," said the fairy. "No doubt other class complainers will soon want one of my spells." With that, she did a back dive into *The Encyclopedia of Fairies* and vanished.

Danny returned the book to its proper place and headed for the library door.

"Daniel," Miss Reed called after him. "I have something special for you."

Danny stopped in his tracks. "Not again," he groaned.

"I laminated some bookmarks," said the librarian. "One for each student in the school."

Danny let out a long breath. The bookmark Miss Reed handed him was red, and although he hated the color red, his only reply was, "Thank you."

"So how was your afternoon at school?" the librarian asked.

"Fine," said Danny. "Nothing to complain about."

The Homework Gnome

The tall teacher sat at his desk, reading from his assignment book. "For homework this weekend, class, do math pages fifty and fifty-one. Also complete the worksheet on contractions I handed out, write ten sentences using words from our spelling list, and look up the five vocabulary words on the board. And don't forget that your book reports are due. Oh, yes, also work on your social studies projects, cut out news articles for Current Events, and collect some fall leaves for an art project. Did everyone get that? Good. Have a fun weekend. You are excused."

The third-graders rose from their seats. They retrieved their backpacks from the coat closet and began stuffing them with math books, spelling books, reading books, dictionaries, and binders. They also packed their lunchboxes, library books, water bottles, notices for parents, baseball mitts, and recorders to practice for music. No wonder most of them grunted when they hoisted the backpacks onto their shoulders.

Hari stood by his desk in the fourth row. After loading his leather pack, he heaved it onto his back, tottering under the weight.

"This thing must weigh more than I do," he said. "My spine will be curved like an S. My shoulders will be stooped forever. I'll have back trouble before I'm ten, all because of *homework!*"

The tall teacher looked up from his desk. "Hari, may I have a word with you?" he said.

Pulling the backpack straps with his thumbs, Hari lumbered to the teacher's desk.

"Hari, according to my records you didn't turn in Tuesday's homework," the teacher said solemnly.

Hari shifted the load on his shoulders. "Well, you see, that night I put my homework papers in my pants pocket," he explained. "My mom washed my pants and my homework ended up looking like Cream of Wheat."

The teacher frowned. "But you didn't turn your homework in on Thursday either."

"Well, you see, I did my homework on the computer that night," said Hari. "Our computer crashed and my homework vanished into cyberspace."

The tall teacher's ears glowed red. "You also didn't turn in your homework this morning," he said.

"Well, you see ...," Hari began.

"Hari, no more excuses," said the teacher. "From now on you'll get your homework done on time. Monday morning all the homework I just assigned will be on my desk. Done, finished, completed.

Understand?"

Hari resisted the urge to make an excuse about the weekend and nodded. Bowed forward, head tilted down, he trudged out of the classroom, muttering to himself, "Homework makes no sense to me. Why must we do schoolwork at home after spending seven hours doing schoolwork in school? Teachers don't even expect kids to like homework. That's why they call it home ... *work!*"

By this time the hall was empty. Halfway down, a drinking fountain stuck out of the wall. Hari stopped for a drink. The weight of his backpack tipped him to one side as he bent toward the faucet.

He had taken only one gulp, however, when a low voice by his feet startled him. "Hey, buddy, take that load off your shoulders. Want to make a homework deal?"

Hari looked down. On the wall underneath the fountain was a vent covered by a wire screen.

"Come down here, buddy," the voice said. "I have an offer you can't refuse." Yes, it came from the vent. "How would you like it if you never had to do homework again?"

How could Hari resist? He plopped his backpack on the floor and dropped to his knees. A warm breeze blew back his hair as he leaned toward the vent.

"Who are you?" he whispered. "What did you mean by a homework deal?"

As Hari spoke the screen swung open. Sitting

inside the square hole, his back against the side with his legs crossed, was a chubby man the size of a math book. He was bald with pointed ears and, judging by his wrinkled face, very old. Dust covered the gray trousers and long gray apron that he wore.

Small, raisin eyes shifted from side to side as the little man talked. "Yes, buddy, I have a homework deal for you. That's why they call me the Homework Gnome."

"The Homework Gnome?" Hari exclaimed. "But I've never heard of you. What do you do?"

The man linked his hands behind his head. The tips of his ears wiggled. "You see, buddy, I live down in the warm, humid boiler rooms of this school," he replied. "I do homework for any student who's willing to pay the price."

"The price? Why, I'd give anything to have someone do my homework for me!" said Hari.

A grin crossed the gnome's round face. "The price, my boy, depends on the homework you need done. Workbook sheets are the cheapest. Social studies and science projects are a bit more. But if you want me to write an essay or book report, expect to pay a premium."

Hari unzipped his backpack and pulled out some books. "See, I have tons of homework to do this weekend, including a book report," he said. "But all I have is sixty-five cents."

Again the gnome's eyes shifted. "Oh, but I never accept money in my homework deals, buddy," he said. "I'll do all your homework if you'll lend me another type of sense, one of your five."

Hari blinked, gulped, and rubbed his ears. Had he heard right? "You mean like my seeing, tasting, feeling, hearing, and smelling?" he asked. "We learned about the five senses in science."

The gnome nodded. "Here's the deal. You lend me one of your five senses on Monday for one hour— you choose the sense and you choose the hour—and I'll have your homework, done, finished, completed, inside your desk that morning. You say your homework makes no sense, buddy? That's why I need one sense from you to make your homework."

Hari thought a moment, but only a moment, before he answered. "Well, I *was* running out of homework excuses. And since my teacher says I don't listen to him during math anyway, why don't you take my hearing that hour. The teacher won't suspect that anything is different."

The gnome stuck out his tiny hand. Hari shook it with his thumb and forefinger. The deal was struck.

All the way home Hari swung his empty backpack in his hand. He thought about all the extra TV he would watch that weekend. "Homework traded for a sense, now *that's* a deal," he told himself.

On Monday morning Hari walked straight to his desk. He threw open the lid. Yes, there sat his books in neat piles. His completed homework papers lay on top, including a two-page book report and five fall leaves for the art project.

Hari brought his homework up to the teacher's desk. "The Homework Gnome does excellent work," he told himself, laying the papers in the IN basket. "I couldn't have done better myself."

By nine o'clock, math period, Hari had almost forgotten his deal with the Homework Gnome. While the tall teacher talked about numerators and denominators, Hari played with eraser crumbs on his desktop. Not until the hour was almost over did he realize his ears weren't working. He couldn't hear a thing, even if he wanted to.

But at ten o'clock the teacher's voice rang out, loud and clear. "Recess time, class!"

"What a great deal I made with the Homework Gnome," Hari said under his breath. "I'd be lucky to meet him again."

Sure enough, as Hari lugged his backpack down the hall that afternoon, the Homework Gnome called from the vent, "Care to make another homework deal, buddy?"

Hari sank to the floor. "Spelling work, an essay, and math pages. What'll it cost me?" he asked.

"Just one more of your senses for an hour," said the gnome, his pointed ears twitching. "You could pay through your nose this time, buddy."

Hari nodded. "Sure, you can have my sense of smell during spelling time. I never need to smell while I spell." Again the pair shook hands, sealing the deal. The next day Hari found the completed homework in his desk once more. Spelling period came, and while Hari rifled through his desk for his spelling book, Kate, who sat nearby, threw up on the floor.

"Ewwwww!" went the third-graders. They held their noses and gagged as Kate rushed from the room.

Hari took a deep breath. "Can't smell a thing," he

boasted. How pleased he was with his second homework deal.

After school the gnome called to Hari a third time. "Another deal, buddy? Another one of your senses for completed homework?"

"I have a social studies project due tomorrow," Hari explained. "I need to make a model of a Sioux teepee. Are you any good at making models?"

"Social studies projects are my specialty," the Homework Gnome replied. "State maps made with papier mâché, forts from toothpicks, or log cabins constructed with sugar cubes, I can do them all. Each of my projects comes with a guaranteed A grade."

Hari was already thinking about the TV programs he could watch after school. "Then you can have my sense of taste during handwriting tomorrow," he said.

To Hari's delight, a teepee made with real sticks and animal hide and painted with authentic Sioux symbols sat on his desk the next morning.

During handwriting, he sucked on the end of his pencil, tasting nothing.

"Yes, life after school has never been better, thanks to the Homework Gnome," he told himself.

Hari's next deal was to

exchange his homework for his sense of touch during lunch. As he sat in the cafeteria, his legs and arms fell asleep. Milk dribbled down his chin when he drank and bread crumbs dropped from his lips when he ate.

"Maybe this time the homework trade wasn't such a good idea," he mumbled.

But no sooner had Hari said this than Richard slugged him on the shoulder.

"Didn't even hurt, Richard," Hari said, smirking. "Do it again. Go ahead. Hit my other shoulder." And that made the entire deal worth it.

The next trade was even trickier. How could Hari give up his fifth sense, his eyesight, for an hour at school? But as he walked down the hall that afternoon, he remembered tomorrow was Friday, and on Friday the class had health.

"Last week during health the teacher showed a video called *Brushing Your Teeth*," he told the gnome. "I slept through the whole thing. Maybe tomorrow I won't need to see that hour either."

For the fifth morning in a row, Hari turned his homework in on time. This week's health video was called *The Four Food Groups*, and while it played, Hari took a refreshing nap. He never even knew his eyesight was gone.

But when school was out, Hari was worried. After dropping his extra-heavy backpack by the vent, he said, "Homework Gnome, this weekend I have a ton of homework. But I'm out of senses for a trade."

The gnome's black eyes flashed, and the tips of his ears wiggled. "I know, buddy, and weekend homework is costly. But you do have another sense, one you never learn about in science."

Hari unzipped his backpack. "Take whatever sense you want as long as I don't have to do this homework," he said. "You can have it during Current Event time on Monday."

Monday morning came. By now Hari was so used to having his homework done for him, he dropped it into the IN basket without a glance.

"Time for Current Events," the tall teacher announced. "Who has some news to report?"

As his classmates talked about what was happening in the world, Hari sat wondering what would happen to him. What sense would the Homework Gnome borrow this time? So far his vision, hearing, tasting, touching, and smelling worked fine.

At the moment, Kate was reading about hailstones the size of softballs that fell in Iowa. Hari was half listening when he did something he had no idea why he did. He stood on his chair and announced, "Ladies and jellyfish! I'm Hari, the Third-Grade Daredevil. I flirt with danger! I laugh at injury! I'll now cross the classroom without once touching the floor!"

The class went dead quiet. All heads turned toward Hari, who had climbed onto his desktop.

"Get down from there before you topple over, Hari," the tall teacher said.

"Nonsense!" Hari declared. And he jumped onto Morgan's desktop, twirled, and leaped onto Kate's.

"Hari, what's gotten into you?" said the teacher. "Have you lost your senses?"

"The cow jumped over the moon! And the dish ran away with the spoon!" Hari shouted.

From Kate's desk he leaped onto George's, twirled again, and sprang onto Joey's desk in the front row. Finally he jumped onto the tall teacher's large metal desk. From there he reached up and began swinging from the overhead light fixtures. "I'm Hari, the Third-Grade Daredevil!" he repeated. "I flirt with danger! I laugh at injury!"

The tall teacher's ears had never been redder. "Hari, get down from there at once! You're going to fall! Use your common sense!"

The words struck Hari like a dodgeball. He dropped onto the teacher's desktop and checked the clock. Now he understood. Now he knew why he was saying and doing such senseless things. The Homework Gnome had indeed borrowed another of his senses, one that Hari had forgotten all about—his common sense.

Crouching, he pulled his homework from the IN

basket and waved it in the air. "I *can't* use my common sense, teacher," he said. "I traded it to a gnome who does my homework for me! I haven't done my own homework all week!"

The tall teacher reached up and hauled Hari off the desktop by the waist. "We'll talk about homework later," he said. "Right now I'm taking you straight to the principal's office."

With Hari tucked under his arm, the teacher stormed from the room.

"Hurrah!" Hari called out. "I can't wait to get to the office! I can't wait to hear what Mr. Principle will say to me!"

Not until the end-of-school bell rang did Hari return to the room at the end of the hall. He sat at his desk, waiting for the lecture he knew he would get.

"Hari, homework might not make sense to you, but teachers assign it for good reason," the tall teacher began. "Students benefit from the structure, organization, and self-discipline that homework requires."

Hari hadn't a clue what this meant, but he nodded anyway.

"From now on, you will do your own homework without excuses," the teacher went on. "I expect your parents to sign each homework paper you turn in. Understand?"

Hari nodded again and stood. Shouldering his backpack, he shuffled out the door.

The Homework Gnome was waiting under the

drinking fountain. "Care to make another home-work deal, buddy?" he called out. "Want to trade your sense of humor or sense of timing? How about your sense of direction, sixth sense, or horse sense?"

Hari yanked on his backpack straps with his thumbs. "Sorry, Homework Gnome, I think I'll have the good sense to go home and get my homework done, finished, completed, all by myself, no matter how torturous it is."

With that, Hari shifted the load on his back. Then, bowed forward, head lowered, he continued down the hall.

Math Rashes

TREEEEEE

The playground was gone. Overnight it had disappeared under a foot of snow as white and flat as a birthday cake. Mr. Leeks, the custodian, was the only person on the playground before school started. He was shoveling the front sidewalk with a wide, curved shovel. The air was cold and snappy. The morning sun sprayed sparkles over the new white world.

At eight-thirty two yellow buses rolled into view. They stopped in front of the school, spraying slush across the sidewalk. The bus doors folded open, and out leaped whooping children, wrapped in knitted caps, thick coats, and rubber boots.

How inviting the snowy playground looked! The students were eager to make snow forts, snow tunnels, and snow angels where only yesterday asphalt and grass had been.

The Playground Lady, however, stood between the buses. Her hands were stuffed into the pockets of a long, quilted coat. The Bad-News Whistle was stuffed between her lips.

Treeeeeeeeeep! the whistle blasted.

"The buses were late today, so head straight inside!" the Playground Lady roared. "Hurry! Hurry! The bell has already rung."

The students plodded into the school. *Tramp! Tramp! Tramp!* One by one they veered from the hallway into their classrooms.

The third-graders headed to the end of the hall. They entered the room cautiously. After hanging up their wraps in the coat closet, they stepped timidly to their seats.

A new person stood by the blackboard. A young woman. A substitute. A teacher who didn't know the classroom rules, the daily routine, or even the students' names.

The substitute was facing the blackboard. Her brown ponytail swayed as she wrote her name in chalk. She wore a red bow in her hair. When she turned she smiled at the class with bright red lips.

"Good morning, kids. My name is Miss Givings," the sub said. "Your teacher is sick today, and I'm so excited to be here. I just finished my student teaching, and this is my first job as a substitute. You kids are my very first class."

Richard grinned, Danny groaned, Andrew began doodling, and Hari said a short prayer about no homework.

Miss Givings took attendance and checked the tall teacher's lesson plan book. "Now, kids, we have lots of schoolwork to do today. Just because you have a substitute doesn't mean anything will be different. First, will you take out your reading books?"

Desktops opened. The class took one last longing look out the window before reading began.

The story was dull, with few pictures, little conversation, and no funny parts. Even worse, the substitute kept interrupting readers by asking, "What does that word mean? Who can explain that sentence? Why do you think that happened?"

Next came handwriting. "Today your teacher wants us to practice writing the hump letters," said the substitute. "Cursive *n*'s, *m*'s, and *h*'s all have humps."

So the third-graders wrote cursive *n*'s, *m*'s, and *h*'s over and over until their fingers ached.

Math followed. "Mathematics is a very important subject, kids," Miss Givings said. "Think of all the math you must do if you go shopping. Think of the careers that will require math when you grow up."

For the next half-hour the class plowed through twenty long subtraction problems with lots of crossing out and borrowing from the thousands place.

"My mom uses a calculator and credit card when she shops," Morgan muttered.

"I'm going to be a soccer player when I grow up," Danny grumbled. "Why do soccer players need to know math?"

All this time the snow beckoned outside the window. Squirming in their seats, the class yearned to go outside and play. Mimi's eyes wandered toward the playground, causing her to write her ones in the tens place. George studied the snowdrift under the windowsill and leaned closer until he nearly fell from his chair.

After math, hope rose when Miss Givings turned toward the window. "Well, kids, doesn't the snow outside look wonderful?" she said. "Think of all the fun you could have in the snow. You could go sledding, skiing, or snowboarding. You could build snowmen, snow tunnels, or snow forts."

The third-graders sat on the edge of their seats, ready to spring to the coat closet.

But instead of releasing her students, the sub picked up some writing paper. "So this morning for creative writing we'll write snow stories," she said.

"Your title should be 'Wonderful Snow.' Now, kids, put on your thinking caps and begin to write. Have fun and let's be creative."

This was too much. At the moment the snow was not wonderful. Inches beyond the glass it was teasing the class, crisp, powdery, and sparkling in the sunlight.

Mimi chewed on her pencil. Richard snarled, ready to call a student strike right there and then. Even Kate, the best writer in the class, couldn't think of a kind word to write about snow.

The substitute strolled up and down the rows of desks, handing out paper. "Don't forget to use the proper story heading," she instructed. "And keep within the margins."

As Miss Givings gave a writing sheet to George, the boy raised a hand to his mouth. *Hic! Hic! Hic!* he went. *Hic! Hic! Hic!* he went again. George had the hiccups.

The substitute checked the seating chart. "George, go to the sink and get a drink of water. Swallow nine times. That's a hiccup cure I learned while student teaching."

George walked to the sink. He slurped some water, gulping once, twice ... three, four, five, six, seven, eight ... nine times. *Hic! Hic! Hic! Hic! Hic!* But he was still hiccuping.

Now Kate, who sat behind George, started to hiccup as well. She held a hand to her lips and looked toward the sub.

"Get a drink, Kate," Miss Givings said. "And remember, swallow nine times."

Kate slurped, gulped, and counted as George had done. Yet she too—*Hic! Hic! Hic! Hic!*—continued to hiccup.

The substitute stopped passing out papers. "How odd," she said. "That hiccup cure has never failed before. Are you sure you each swallowed nine times, not eight or ten?"

George and Kate nodded and hiccuped some more.

At this point *Hic! Hic! Hic!* erupted from Gabrielle in the fourth row, and *Hic! Hic! Hic!* came from Danny sitting catty-corner from her.

Mimi's hand flew into the air. "Miss Givings, whenever I get the hiccups, my mom tells me to hold my breath and count to one hundred."

George, Kate, Gabrielle, Danny, and Morgan, who was now hiccuping also, sucked in some air and counted. But—*Hic! Hic! Hic!*—this cure worked no better.

"Miss Givings, I read that you should breathe into a paper bag," Hari suggested. "Don't use a plastic bag. Only paper, in and out, in and out."

By now, five more third-graders had the hiccups. They each found a paper lunch bag in the coat closet and began blowing into it.

Meanwhile, Richard sneaked up behind two hiccupers. "Boo!" he shouted. "Boo! Boo!"

They jumped an inch.

"Did I spook you? Did I?" Richard asked. "Scaring people always makes hiccups go away." Then he crept around the classroom startling anyone he could.

Miss Givings leaned against the teacher's desk, shaking her head. "How odd. The hiccups seem to be spreading around the room," she said. "If I didn't know better I'd say they were contagious. What can I do? I never learned about contagious hiccups in teacher's college."

Joey in the first row called out, "I saw a sure cure for hiccups on TV, Miss Givings. Everybody should hop up and down and twirl at the same time."

Andrew disagreed. "The newspaper said that the best way to get rid of hiccups is to stand on your head."

While some third-graders hopped and twirled, others did headstands. Some continued to gulp water and others held their breath. Yet, despite all these sure cures, every student in the classroom at the end of the hall soon had the hiccups.

Hic! Hic! Hic! Hic! The classroom sounded like popcorn popping in a pan.

Danny held his middle. "I've been hiccuping so much my gut aches," he complained.

Morgan flopped into her chair. "I don't know which is more exhausting, hiccuping or the hiccup cures," she said.

The substitute checked the lesson plan book. "But you kids must stop hiccuping," she said. "We still have stories to write. We must do our vocabulary, social studies, S.S.R., and read our *Weekly Readers.*"

Hic! Hic! Hic! Hic! Hic! Hic! the third-graders answered, louder than before.

At this point a scream came from the fourth row. "There are spots on my arms," Morgan called out. "No, they're not spots; they're plus and minus signs! My arms are covered with plus and minus signs!" She began scratching the red math symbols that covered her hands and arms. The odd rash quickly spread over her neck and face.

"Spots are on my arms too," Hari suddenly called out. "They're numbers! *Hic! Hic! Hic!* Miss Givings, I'm covered with the numbers zero to nine!"

Soon afterward Kate announced, "Yikes! Now I have red spots on my arms! They're times and division signs! And numbers! Yikes! Entire math problems are breaking out all over me!"

Miss Givings sat on her desktop. "How odd! Math Rashes!" she exclaimed. "During student teaching I learned what to do about bee stings, mosquito bites, and poison ivy bumps, but never about Math Rashes."

By now most of the third-graders had slumped in their seats, exhausted, heads still bouncing with hiccups. Danny scratched some equal signs on his forehead, and Richard scratched the decimal points on his belly.

The substitute walked up and down the aisles, examining her students as a doctor might her patients. "Hiccups and Math Rashes. Hiccups and Math Rashes," she said over and over. "This can mean only one thing—an allergy. Kids, I believe you've had an allergic reaction to something, something in this classroom. But what could it be? You haven't eaten anything. You haven't touched anything. How can we cure this allergy and get back to our schoolwork?"

Hic! Hic! Hic! Hic!

Mimi's hand went up. "Miss Givings, I think the allergy has something to do with schoolwork," she called out. "Whenever you mention it, I hiccup more."

"And my Math Rash itches worse," said Andrew, scratching the fractions on the back of his neck.

Miss Givings raised a hand to her chin. "Yes, yes, I see what you mean." As an experiment she suddenly announced, "Time for a pop math quiz, kids!"

Hic! Hic! Hic! More hiccups and scratching.

"Yes, that explains it," the substitute said. "That's what's causing your hiccups and Math Rashes, all right. I believe this entire class has become allergic to, of all things, schoolwork! Yes, this is a Schoolwork Allergy. I've given you an overdose of schoolwork this morning, haven't I? You've had too much reading, too much writing, and especially too much arithmetic. So you all broke out in Math Rashes. Isn't that right? Oh, there's so much about teaching I still need to learn, kids, but I think I know a cure for this allergy." Here Miss Givings looked out the window again. "Your next assignment is to go outside in the snow and play. Now, no arguing about it. No more school-work for now. Put on your wraps at once and march straight to the playground."

Within minutes the third-graders were outside in the glorious snow. Soon the playground resembled the cratered surface of the moon. The students built snow forts and supplied them with snowballs. They dropped on their backs to make snow angels and stomped around the soccer field writing their names in giant letters.

Miss Givings, wrapped in a long red coat, red beret, and red scarf, stood by the jungle gym. She packed a snowball and started rolling it toward the center of the playground. When it was the size of a globe, two third-graders helped push it until it stood taller than they were. Now the entire class joined in. They rolled another boulder slightly smaller than the first, then another smaller still. Soon they were standing around the tallest snowman W. T. Melon Elementary School had ever seen. It wore a red scarf and red beret.

"Is everyone having a good time, kids?" the substitute called out. "This play should cure your Schoolwork Allergy. Isn't it fun out here? I think I'll enjoy being a teacher very much. Does everyone feel better now?"

The class answered with whoops and cheers. And not once during the entire recess time did anyone hear a single hiccup or scratch a single Math Rash.